NIGHT WOLVES

Yulalona Lopez

NIGHT WOLVES

Tracking the Elusive Wolves of the Balkans

Yulalona Lopez

Calliope Press
Sarasota
2010

Acknowledgments
*Old Wolf Song, Wolf News, Lightbearer, Passions of Wolf,
Wolf Loves to Hide,* by A. M. Caratheodory

Photographs: Mandrata horses (page 15), Snow tracking (17),
Dancing at Rosaritsa (20), Wolf mating scene (23), Pig bones
(28), Tracking on roads (32), Dead wolf (35), Wolf print (38),
Wolf scat (40), Bear den (43), Bear print (48), Field above the
blind (49), Sheep (53), Sofia bus station (55), Boiling traps (60),
Salamander (62), Trapline (65), Yulalone returning (71), Arul
(72), Storm beginning (79), King and Queen rocks (81), Fox
peak (83), Snail (87), Last survey (93), Snake-Lizard (94), Black
Stork (100).

This Calliope Press Edition of *Night Wolves*
is Published by Three Muses Books, M&RW

Prepared and produced by Calliope Press, Boston
Designed by Rian Ektropic Designs, Cortez
Please address all correspondence for the M&RW, Ltd.,
Calliope Press, SynGeo, or Rian Ektropic Designs to:
    Post Office Box 370,
    Tallevast, Florida 34270-0370
    1-941-447-7470
    editor@3muses.us

Yulalona: lopez@itsayaya.com

Second Printing
ISBN 0-911385-52-5
    978-0-911385-52-6

Printed in the USA

Contents

Waiting for Wolves 9
First Sign
Running Figures
Tasting Essences
Night Blind
Testing Waters
Window on Wolves
Seeing Blind
Tracking Stories
Dancing at the Rosaritsa
Carrying Corn Treats
Ties that Bind
Ambiguous Prints
The Bear
Dawn Finds Bones
Teasing the Trackers

Following Wolves 33
Karakachans
Circling Sites
Crossing Borders
The Gypsy's Curse
In the Hide of the Wolf
Daylight Equals Death
Shadow Play
Landscape with Horses
Digging Badger
Black Peak
Black Butterflies
Black Woodpecker Playing Tag
Climbing

Night Wolves 45
Green Shapes
Brown Bear Prints
Freezing
Wild Horses
Lost Between Villages
Caged Wolf

Speaking for Wolves
Arul Mountain
Embracing Metal
Making Lines
Guns and laws
Empty Traps
More Empty Traps
Always Empty Traps
Last Chance
Counting Wolves

Lost in the Wild   **73**
Prelude to Dying
Tri-Color Paths
Howling
Wild Cat Ghost
Snow Blind
Chess Pieces
Sun on Snow
Fox Peak
Watching Chamois
Tracking the Tracker

Imaginary Wolves   **88**
Waiting for Wolves
Passion of Wolves
Old Wolf Song
Wolf News
Song of the Shepherd
Song of the She-Wolf
The Biologist's Plan
Still Snake
Alpha Reasoning
Howling
Claw Marks
Passions of Wolf
Seeing Light
Lightbearer
Wolf Loves to Hide

Author/Colophon   100

Author's Note

This book is based on several wolf research projects and on the experiences of several Peace Corps volunteers, as well as the work of numerous Bulgarian, Romanian, Greek, and Russian rangers and scientists. The people, places, and wildlife are all real. Since this is a work of fiction, however, they will not be named. I trust the spirit of this book is to their liking, although it is hard to capture the real excitement, adventure, and fun.

Dedication

To Legend (*Canis lupus irremotus X*), Francisco (*Canis lupus baileyi*), Mariya (*Canis Lupus lupus*), Peyto (*Canis lupus lupus*), and the incredibly secretive wolves of the Balkans. It is hard to describe any of you in words, but I know you by your scent, sounds, and your trails.
I am lonely and so much poorer without you.

And, to the following humans (*Homo sapiens sapiens*):
Alan, Aleksander, Anton, Boyko, Damian, Dimitor, Elena, Gencho, Ivan, Kamen, Klementine, Kosta, Kostadin, Lalyo, Marcella, Maria, Mitko, Nela, Nikolai, Pavel, Petur, Sava, Sidar, Valya, Vyara, Xristo, and many unrecognized others.
I miss all of you also.

Waiting for Wolves

First Sign

Before dawn. After four hours of walking
uphill   we reached the far western edge
of the park. As we walked up the valley,
we passed three harvest sites, each with a narrow
eroding lane pointing directly up the slope.
Then we turned directly upwards and pulled
ourselves up the steep hillside,
hand over hand, using roots and branches.

From a peak, we looked down
on harvest patchworks, with damaged
trees standing and tracks eroding to mud
plains. We went down by hand and stopped
on a plateau. I found a bear tree, with claw marks
two meters above the ground and light
coarse hairs in the sap. Bulchru found
a tree with marks three meters off
the ground. The same bear we guessed.

To get lower down the vertical slope,
we fell from tree trunk
to tree trunk. There were many
footprints from elk and a few rootings
by wild swine. Bulchru found a wolf track—
our first—
on the road by an old house,
a house where cheese-makers had worked
    decades ago.
We followed the tracks as they swerved
to investigate a puddle with many elk
tracks in it and around it.   There were two
wolves, now, one much smaller. The larger
track was index-finger-wide and long. We lost
the trail in the dry grasses. The sun
was high, so we decided to break on the field
in the grasses. Bulchru sat smoking
while I lay down and dozed
in the warm October sun. A bee

collected clover pollen around
my head, quietly gathering it, then buzzing
madly to get to the next heavy
blossom. I noticed Bulchru was sleeping,
    suddenly a crash
from the beech forest below—
tree falling or bear tripping—we got up
immediately and walked downhill.   It took
two hours to get back down
hill. A jeep with Andrei was waiting
on the road   both were smoking.

Running Figures

I caught the dawn bus to the village
Vidima, close to the Park, to meet
with Bulchru and Trifon. Bulchru had the jeep
again. So, we drove eight kilometers
to the old water works station, Vets.
    Trifon and I went up the west
side of the river and Bulchru decided
to walk on the other side three hundred
meters away. We lost sight of him
after five minutes in the trees. The trees
had lost all their leaves and their grey beech
bark made the forest look ghostly as well
as slightly dirty. The snow got deeper
as we walked along animal trails.

Heard a bellowing, answered
by another fainter one farther up
the hill. Trifon guessed the first one
was Bulchru. We stopped and watched
the opposite hill.   The forest was still.
After five minutes I saw two forms
running down towards the river. They ran well
in the snow. I wondered if they were wolves
or dogs, but Trifon, who had sharper
    eyes, said that they were roe
deer. We watched them until they were out
of sight.   As we continued to walk,

we came upon several places where deer
had bedded for the night, on a deer-body
depression in the snow, there were urine stains
on one end and nose marks on the other.
In the snow nearby small tufts of grass
were exposed. We could not resolve the scene
   in the Bulgarian language. My lack.
Finally, we were all the way up at the head wall
of the river. No signs of wolves or bears.

Tasting Essences

Climbing near the top of the next
ridge we found a wildlife trail
in fifty centimeters of snow with fresh
   wolf prints which we followed
for a while. Near a clearing the wolf
   had vomited: Blades of grass,
one leaf, two large bits of roe deer hide
in yellow stomach acids—
I could not help but taste this
to see what was bad. Trifon grimaced.
We measured the size and distance
of the prints and discussed the circumstance.
The paw prints seemed small and only sank
into the snow maybe seventeen centimeters
with a shorter stride, but, they were proportioned
right. Later, I found out why
   she was sick
         and vomited it back up.
We continued to follow the tracks
as they crossed a rabbit's
then veered in and out of the cover
of a small silver fir nursery
and into the white field
   and there was no sign
that the two ever met in the flesh.

I had some peanuts from my pocket
I used to cover the taste
of bad deer.

    Heard an elk snuffling
in the snow and headed that way.
The snow had been pawed aside
to reach the brown grasses from fall.
Heard the woodpeckers knocking on beeches
    then saw all three, small with white
and black and a few red feathers.

I found a bed where a roe deer had recently
slept, then urinated to the side. Within
a few meters
          two more beds
cleaner and whiter. I followed
those tracks up the hill.
Two bird shapes between trees.

We lost the tracks over the side
of the ridge. It was mid-morning and Trifon noted
that we had hit the end of a loop
and should start back. We had gone two ridges
away. The walk was easy to start
we were in a field with a meter of snow, but no
rocks or trees. As we plowed along
the ridge, it got rockier. Then we went
          straight
down through the trees for a few kilometers,
slipping on wet rocks, branches and leaves
          under the snow.

At the water station, Trifon set off a firecracker
to let Bulchru know we were back,
but Bulchru was inside already eating
lunch. The stove had made it warm so we took
off a layer of clothes and shoes.
Trifon fixed a sandwich. I had peanuts and tea.
I asked for a piece of cheese
and bread. He replied, "Friendship is friendship,
but cheese is cheese."
I understood that I had to bring my own food.
    The guard, who lived there,
Zhan, returned from his rounds and found

us at lunch; we talked about the snow.   I looked
around the room, at two beds, a desk,
and a stove. Shelves on two walls, one had a stereo
and a small rock. After an hour of cheese and friendship
we decided to slog back to the village.

The Night Blind
Andrei and Bulchru picked me up before
the early bus. In the headlight's cone
We saw a fox cross the road. We drove
past an old strawed house and up behind it—
it was an old logging road leading
to the forestry land. It was badly eroded
and limited us to five kilometers
an hour. We bottomed out twice and twice
    had to inspect the suspension. As they smoked,
I looked for signs. It would have been faster
to walk, but we were obligated to use the technology.
The road went along the ridge overlooking
the village, so it was always in sight.

Finally we were on top of another ridge,
where Bulchru and I had seen wolf prints
earlier. Now it was drier and there were fewer
    prints, one from a wolf
and maybe two from dogs. The dog prints
were smaller, with shorter nails, and they wandered
aimlessly; a wolf was not as wasteful
of energy and time. The mud hole was drying
up. Bulchru said it marked a major wildlife
trail going east into Severen Djendem.
As I looked in all directions, I saw two places
that might work for a night blind. The first
    was a beech tree on the side
of the hill about a hundred meters away;
we walked there. The tree had three stems,
the third broken off about three meters in the air
it could hold a platform. The second
candidate was an old shepherd's hut about the same
elevation. It sat on a broken concrete pad

13

and the roof was made of overlapping
slices of old rubber tires. It would need an opening
to see the trail from that angle. I agreed
reluctantly that it would be easier to fix
than to build a new platform in the tree to hide on.

Then we drove higher through a meadow
and over a ridge to an abandoned
cheese factory, but it was not abandoned,
just reduced to three men making
cheese and yogurt. They asked if we wanted
some, and we did. Bulchru started
helping two younger men rinse curds
through cheese cloth. The older man Sidar
led Andrei and I into the building, which framed
the mountains in broken windows.
　　Four rooms with beds. A fifth set up
with a stove. The fire was hot and soup
was steaming. We sat at a long wooden
table; on it was a bowl of soup with dead flies—
and hundreds of living flies, waiting
for the next delivery. Other bowls were overturned
on the table. Bringing the yogurt in a blue
plastic bucket Sidar ladled out a liter
for each of us, into two of the dishes
that had been overturned. Quite good, I commented
and was told it was from sheep. I had seen
ten cows on the way up but no sheep, so
I asked where they were.　　Higher
pasture, all two hundred.　Bulchru and the guys
came back with a bowl of burned fat
and a bowl of tomatoes. Bulchru cut
the tomatoes and Sidar dowsed
them with salt and olive oil. Two loaves of bread
appeared. I had a hunk with water. Everyone else
dove into the fat and tomatoes. After an hour
of gossip about the park and the weather,
we said we had to go look for poachers
and fires. So, we thanked them and left.
The trip back was just as long and slow.

Testing Waters

I hiked the trail by the waterhole alone. The roads
were covered with snow, and large potholes
    were filled with icy water. So,
I finally learned to walk along the edges.
This was the first time I had walked this way,
along the road, not on the trails
or directly up the slopes—deer and bear
only went directly up to escape
being caught, preferring cross-slope
trails they made or even human roads. Humans
wrecked their way in, but that made moving
easier for everyone. The road took longer
but the grade was gentler
and there was no chance of getting lost.
A few tracks of mice, deer, and fox.
And then presently-free horses.

I climbed the broken beech and sat
a while, but realized I could not sleep
in the crotch. More tracks around the pond.
It was cloudy, so the night scope did not work.
That meant that I could get more sleep. The sleeping
bag between the roots of the tree was comfortable.
I only stayed in it for an hour at a time
and observed for the other hour. I decided after all
to make a window for the shepherd's hut.

Window on Wolves

I asked one of the rangers, Dimitor, for help, so
he took me to a local sawmill, where the operator
agreed to make a small four-paned window
to my specs. When it was ready, he drove
to my home with it. We discussed when
I should pay the two cases of beer
for it, but not before Friday or the workers
would get drunk and not come to work.

Andrei arrived at the door and I showed him
the window. Pencho came over and we went
to the hardware store for nails.
        I did not have to pay; later
I found out that Pencho gave the owner
two bottles of brandy from his home-still.

Then Andrei mentioned that he had no tools,
and he did not know if Bulchru did, so we walked
to his house to borrow a hammer and saw.
    We walked back to the sawmill
and Petko finished a few pieces
of wood that would work to slide
the window on, and we loaded it all in the jeep.

Andrei and I drove to Bulchru's house.
He was waiting with a new chainsaw
and a double-bladed ax. Then we drove the goat trail,
with the four-wheel-drive in low, past
the meadows near the night blind. We sketched
in the window with a pencil. Bulchru chainsawed
the outer wall to fit the window; his eye
was good and he barely touched the frame.
I hammered nails into the bottom
of the slide frame, but Bulchru took
it outside and squared one of the unfinished sides
with his ax. Then Andrei finished nailing it in place.
        Then Andrei took over the hammer
and finished the bottom slide. I started the top
piece but Bulchru took it away and nailed the other
slide piece to it. I held it while he nailed

into the frame. Then Andrei cut old wood
for a sill.   The window worked.

We walked over to the spring and had a picnic.
I had bread and peanuts, Andrei had bread,
and Bulchru had bread, cheese, tomatoes, apples,
fruit spread, canned meat, and water. Then
we explored, parallel to the trail, for
a while, noticing a few wolf signs, before making
the two-hour trip back to the village.

Seeing Blind

The next day, I took the noon bus to Vidima
and from there walked alone to the blind.
There was more snow than last month,
so I got bogged down, but I made it
before sunset.
    There were the usual assortments
of tracks along the road, but this snow was wet
and heavy. One set of wolf tracks
        crossed the road
and went into the forest. I followed a way
until the vegetation got too low;
it looked like a regular trail. Approaching
the blind, I found more prints around
        the water hole,
still covered with snow, wild pig and roe
deer.   Dusk took forever to turn. I took out
the binoculars, nightscope, knife, camera, and water
and lined them up so I could find them
in the dark. Immediately I heard an owl,
        who doubtless came
to see if I would scare out any mice.

Little activity in the nightscope.
The moon was out, but behind clouds.
        There was a little snow
coming down. The blind seemed too far
from the water hole. With binoculars I saw shadows
that later I found were several wild pigs, very

17

large. I managed to doze for an hour
every other hour, sleeping on the wooden part
of the floor, using my coat as a pillow. Remembering
those wildlife videos I wondered
     if I was ever going to get a good photo
much less a video. Not being
able to sleep much, I left at first light and walked
downhill. I did not stop to take photographs
since I saw no new tracks, other than fox
and roe deer, the most active. I reached Vidima
in time for the eight o'clock bus to Aprilci.

Tracking Stories

Some days later, Dimitar and Gavril, the biologist
and veterinarian who headed the old
     wolf survey project, waited
in an old Lada. We drove through Stokite
     to Lugat, the forestry unit
at the edge of the Park. Hard snow
made the driving risky and slow—fortunately
few other cars were on the road. Dimitar
said that if it was like this tomorrow,
we could forget having a good wolf survey.

At Lugat, we were met by Xristo, a ranger
who led us to the hunting lodge. We were
last to arrive. The others had started drinking
and eating. We sat and drank, and smoked
and talked, for a few hours over salads. Gavril
lectured on wolf tracks and measurements, claiming
that the proportion could be used to tell sex
and age. I added comments on wolf biology
and behavior. Afterwards, we had meat
and potatoes with wine, beer, coke, and homemade
brandy—until well into the next day. The room
we shared was very warm because
the floors were heated; the sleeping bags held
the heat. The bathroom, however, was freezing cold
and there was no hot water.

The next morning, it was snowing
and had been for some time. Half
a meter of new snow. We had cheese
and bread for breakfast, then broke into two
groups of four and piled into two Lada
jeeps. Dimitar, Andrei, Georgiu,
     and I went to investigate
one part of the region, while Bulchru, Xristo,
Gavril, and Young Dimitar went to another.

After driving for forty minutes on a forestry
road, we stopped every time a track
crossed the road. At the third stop we found
a wolf print on the road, the snow filling
it in as we watched. Less than an hour old.
     With Dimitar leading, we left the car
on the road and followed the trail
up hill into the woods. Soon, three more sets
     of prints joined up—hard
to tell because wolves efficiently walked
in each other's tracks. The trails followed a roe deer
throughout the forest, separating and recombining
regularly. At one point they had flushed a deer
towards one of the young males, but he could
not catch her. I followed those tracks myself while

the others stayed together. The deer was leaping
through the snow but the wolf did not break
into a run, only a walk and then a lope,
so they must have decided 'no chase.' Near
a field the trails of the four wolves converged
again, but, after an hour, we lost the prints
in low undergrowth.

After walking back to the jeep, we drove
up to the end of the road. From there we hiked
straight up the mountain side. Finally, we reached
    a meadow, where a group of red deer
had bedded for the night.
The piss and excrement were encased
in ice and snow. We tracked a few more roe deer
but saw no more wolf prints.

In the late afternoon we met the other
group, who had seen only
    an old bear print. Then we returned to the lodge
and had cheese and bread. It was still
snowing, but very lightly.
With cheese, we bribed the Karakachan sheep dog
to walk in the snow and we measured the footprint,
which was demonstrably different from a wolf's,
thinner in the pads even though
the dog was much heavier, seventy kilograms.
    We all took naps for an hour,
then Georgiu and I examined the night scope
while Andrei got the pay
together for the rangers. Dinner started, with a salad
and rakia first. Over fried cheese,
Chicken kabobs and kebabche we discussed
the findings and the plan
for tomorrow. We had intended to go to Tuzia
to train the next group of rangers
on the south side, but with snow hiding signs,
we decided to postpone the tracking.

During the ride back, we discussed kinds of excrements
and what they meant. I had not seen

the licorice kind, which resulted from gorging
on the red meat of deer, but only the hairy
kind, which came from scavenging or eating
small animals like mice with bones and fur.
I suggested that the wolves have not done well
this winter. Dimitar had seen the licorice sort, but
not this year. We discussed the pack sizes
and the mean age of wolves shot
by hunters and shepherds.

Dancing at the Rosaritsa

Next week, Dimitar drove us
to Lugat. He dropped us off at the Rosaritsa
Hotel, closed in the winter
deep in the forest. We dropped
        off the bags and took a hike
up the hill, looking for animal signs. We passed
eight horses and nine cows, but found no other
tracks. It was snowing steadily. Not even a crow
or roe deer broke silence. We returned
but few other rangers had arrived. We sat down
and the four of us talked and drank rakia.

I admired Svetislav's new winter coat. He said
that every ranger got one—they were from Austria
and cost six hundred Leva each. I asked
for a coat for myself and was told
none were left. I looked down at the cotton jacket
that I had worn in the last blizzard. He said
no money at all for wolf surveys,
even though the legislature now required
monitoring for biodiversity. Everyone was better
dressed and better equipped than I was, I complained.
Someone started playing Bulgarian songs,
and everyone started to dance, even me, in the long
never-ending line of the hora. Xristo gave me
a lecture on not trying too hard to change
things. I just wanted to be warm. Time to sleep.

The
hora

The hotel and water were unheated, but wool blankets.
Breakfast was cheese and wine, with bread and tea.
After an hour of joking about drinking the wine,
we all wandered around. Then we left, postponing
the survey again. It was still snowing
and the trip back to the village
     took many hours. The roads
were one-lane, most of the way. The streets
of Stokite were cleanly plowed, unlike most villages.

Carrying Treats

I had set up another survey the next week and the rangers
had agreed to go. I took the early bus to Vidima
and was met by Hassan. Dimitar walked over
with Bulchru and the four of us drove to another
Forestry unit. The snow was melting and very
icy; the car got stuck a few times, and we pushed
it out. When we got to a large hunting blind
we put out some corn. A dead sheep had been dragged
onto the road by some animal but not eaten.
I found no bear, wolf, or even dog tracks.

Hassan and Dimitar put on skis and Bulchru
and I struggled with snowshoes—new, hi-tech fiber
shoes. We slogged up hill for an hour, easily
beating the skiers. Dumped our rucksacks full of corn
on the snow, near a salt lick, to feed the animals

that were doing the best. Going downhill
the skiers easily beat us. It was hard to breathe
because my lungs were frozen.

We drove the Lada to Vets, and put
on chains. Drove up towards the river headwall.
     The car almost got stuck again
but it pulled itself out. Finally, we unloaded
at the old barn, which had finally fallen under
the snow load. I grabbed the food pack
and the others divided up the ninety-kilogram
load of corn. We hiked up to the last hunting
blind, which was next to the Central Balkan Park
and put out the corn. Then we hiked up to the water
containment, where we went into
a small house, started a fire and had lunch.

I brought peanuts, sunflower seeds
and chocolate, Hassan bread, Dimitar half
a bread, and Bulchru an entire kitchen, including
jars of meats, cheeses, cabbage, mayo, milk,
and the ever-popular pure fat cubes. Hassan
planned to stay for a day or two. After
lunch we hiked down for an hour, drove
for forty minutes, and took off the chains
at the water plant. We talked to the workers, had tea
with them, then drove for more tea at the Center Cafe.

Ties that Bind
Doctor Dimitar Hubchev, the archetypical
expatriate Russian scientist, picked me up in his car
to drive to Pavel Banya. Georgiu and one ranger
were driving from Gabrovo, while the section head
and three rangers were driving from Tuzha.
     The hizha had nine beds in one
room, so we had not asked any of the other women
rangers to go. The Minister did not show up. So,
we drove for three kilometers to Skobelovo.
     From there, we all drove
in the two jeeps to the forestry enterprise

house. It had water but no electricity.
We fixed a dinner of marinated cabbage,
peanuts, and kyufte, washed down with brandy
and homemade red wine. The house
had two bedrooms, each with three beds
and a small wood stove. The kitchen had
a wood stove and counter; a sink but
no water. The dining room had one long table
in front of a bench on three walls, where three
more people could sleep, and a large stone fireplace.
There was no toilet or outhouse. We were told to walk
at least one hundred meters away,
so I found a nice tree. As the night went on,
however, the rangers walked less far
and the perimeter became mined with human scat.
We drank past midnight, then slept.

A shape woke us at four; I said three hours
of sleep was not enough. We had tea and drove
along the river. The road was made of gravel
with some large rocks and boulders. We drove
straight up the mountain until the road ended.
As we neared the end, I saw nine dark shapes
　　　moving down the slope towards
the road. I always looked far ahead to see
　　if we startled any wildlife
with our roaring Russian jeeps. Wolves I thought,
and shouted "stop" instead of "look,"
having forgotten the correct word in Bulgarian.
We stopped and watched.
A herd of wild swine, with seven young piglets,
all black. They crossed the road ahead
of us. We got out, walked and looked. As
we were measuring their footprints, we saw
　　　wolf prints. We measured
them and then photographed them—from a male,
female, and two yearlings. The rangers followed,
but I backtracked them, down a talus slope
and into the beech forest where I lost
them in the leaves. It was freezing, and the trees
　　　were all covered with rime

which dropped on me as I walked. Back above,
we followed the tracks along on old logging
road. Pig tracks, roe deer, red deer,
and fox tracks, as well, then a mountain hare
track. Quite a wild highway. The old road
became a path, which Gavril and three others
followed; the rest of us followed the tracks
into the woods, uphill. After a few hundred
meters we lost the tracks, but then found them
again, only now they were coming downhill
and only two not four sets.
So, we followed them through the leaves.
Snow had filled under the trees, but it was
intermittent. Then, we found excrement from one
of the cubs—it was half size; it indicated red meat,
so we thought they had made a kill
recently. Then we lost the tracks again, but kept
walking up above the treeline.

Survey 3

There, we found another set of two larger
tracks; the parents must have ditched the cubs
for a romantic evening alone. The tracks started
out straight but soon indicated that the wolves
    were playing,
running around each other, or rather
the male was racing downhill or uphill

then circling back to the female. This
went on for a few kilometers. I tracked the lower
hill, and Dimitar the upper. I found a place where mating
might have taken place, where two
        wolves had stood
in a tie. The tracks were in a semi-circle. I knelt
and let my imagination recreate the scene.

The tracks moved together down into a forested
glen, where one ranger thought they had a den.
Dimitar had seen another den another ridge
away, at the foot of an Austrian pine, but did not
know this area. I asked that we not follow
them, now, just note the location on the computer; we all
agreed. After a brief lunch of cheese
and salami at a logging landing, we tracked
a deer downhill into the woods. We startled a red
deer, then a roe deer—both ran from us.

After seven hours, we hiked down hill
and were met by the river by the two jeeps; the other
group had found only bear tracks and had gone
to get the jeeps. Near dark, we headed back
to the house, to bean soup, pork
and worst cooked in the fireplace.

Ambiguous Prints

The next day we drove west and directly
into the mountains. It was cold but clear.
The road ended after an hour, so we stopped
and divided into two groups. Gavril took one group
and went parallel around the mountain; Dimitar lead
us directly up the mountain. Finally, past
the tree line and into snow, we found one set
of old tracks, but the snow was hard
and icy. Pencho thought they were wolf,
Dimitar thought jackal, and I thought fox. We each
delivered our arguments. I was sure, since
I had found perfect fox prints before in better
        snow, and measured

them. But, there was reasonable doubt.
The tracks could have been from a small female
wolf, distorted by snow. Jackals rarely visited
mountains, but the size was right.
Only one animal, we agreed.

At the crest we saw two wild goats,
with their dark winter coats. We watched them
for an hour and rested. I found a flat
rock to stretch out on. Clouds passed.
Then, we reached the peak and headed down
the other side, angling towards the jeeps.
In the distance we could see the other
group, eating and goofing off.

After an hour of driving we met
at the Pavel Banya intersection and played
musical cars. The three scientists took the wagon
    and left. One ranger drove back to Tuzha
and one waited for a bus. We five remaining
piled into one jeep, with our full packs. We drove
to Kazanluk, dropped off Mitko at the train station
and Pencho at the center. Then Georgiu, Dimitar,
and I drove to Gabrovo, through Shipka pass,
with snow on the north side but not on the south.

The Bear

The next week, we loaded up two jeeps with ten
observers and drove up the mountain to the forestry
hut. The road meandered across
    the Gabrovsko River, the boundary
between the forestry units and the park. This
is where we had stayed
for the previous survey. We unloaded the jeeps
into the hut. The hut no longer had water
as the stream had dried up; it was way off the grid
and had no electricity, but the rangers brought
a generator and hooked it up to the light
bulb wires in the kitchen and dining room.
I mentioned to Hubchev that three hours of light

remained, so he said good idea, then sat
down with Dimitar to drink coffee
and talk. I left on foot, crisscrossing
      the road for tracks. After an hour, the jeep roared
up and stopped. I got in, but we stopped
every hundred meters to look at tracks.

When we turned a corner, a brown bear
was standing in the road. She ran up the hill
three meters as Dimitar stood
on the brakes; we piled out like a circus team
and stared at her—
she stared back, her face much lighter brown
than her dark brown body. She grunted
and turned up the hill. She stopped
and faced us again, uncertain of our numbers.
We were frozen in place. She turned again
wuffed up the hill and over the ridge.
My camera was in my hand
        forgotten. I moved slowly
      up hill to see her tracks, almost
unrecognizable in the forest floor duff.

We looked around and saw a mouse, then
a hawk. Then drove up to where we saw the wolf
prints last month. I saw another
mouse and two sets of red deer tracks. Another
hour of looking and we returned.

The other rangers had finished preparing
dinner and were eating the salad and drinking
the rakia when we walked in. We sat and had
the same. From three salad plates
and two bread plates, we ate by taking
out food with our forks. We drank straight from
the bottles. Then, one of the young rangers
        came in and started to grill
      pork in the fireplace. Six at a time, putting
the cooked ones in a pot. He served them all
at once, and we ate and talked until late.

Dawn Finds Bones

Breakfast was leftovers, from the same plates
as the night before; the rangers lathered
their bread with mayonnaise, then added cheese
and pieces of meat. We divided into two groups
and packed carefully into the jeeps, driven
by Dimitar and Dimitar, who tried to pass
each other on the dirt roads leading up
the mountain. What other animal could roar
    that loudly and recklessly?

At the final fork, we went north
and they turned south. At the end
of the road, we parked
and hiked directly up the mountain.
As usual, my body protested, heart pounding
and lungs wheezing air. So, I stopped dramatically
and scanned the area with binoculars.
    Suddenly I saw a furtive shape
on the ridge, and whispered to Dimitar
that it was a large mammal, a wolf
perhaps. As we all looked, three other
shapes followed and resolved themselves
into a small herd of roe deer. After a moment,
they saw us and raced away. We kept climbing
to the ridge, which emptied out above
the treeline. We saw patches of snow
and ambled over to look for tracks—old
tracks, old and melted. Roe deer, red deer.
I kept going to the summit and I could see
villages in the distance. We had crossed
the divide from south to north.

We noted deer scat and kept looking
for wolf tracks. None. Headed across
a few ridges to an old pasture with a shepherd's
lean-to. Next to it were rows and rows
of concrete pilings—holding a shed
for cows many years ago and nothing was left
but the pilings. The other group came over
a ridge and ran down to join us. We looked

at the map and planned out another pincher
movement around a hill that might have
a wolf den on the side. Dividing
into two groups, we marched down hill
and then around the entire hill, maybe six
kilometers. Just then, between two firs,
    we found the torn carcass
of a female, two-year-old wild swine;
tooth marks on the bones, and only one hind
foot remained attached to the legs, rib cage
and spine. A meter uphill was a fresh pile
of wolf scat filled with swine hair—I realized
that last night we also had pig to eat. I wondered
if we smelled the same, so I pissed discretely
near the edge of the trail to let them know
the smell of the nosy humans who stepped
in their tracks and pried apart their scat
        to see what they ate.

Dimitar finds a recent wolf kill

The others arrived as we pried and measured
the evidence. As a group we moved
directly up the next mountain. I had recovered
my wind, so climbed faster. Making eye contact
with Dimitar, with his movie-star looks,
    I realized it was to be a race!

Eight bodies churning uphill through
sharp rocks and bushes. I plotted
a smoother course and was second
only to Boleslav, a young ranger.
Dimitar was third, but as we walked
along the ridge looking for tracks, he redeemed
himself by setting the fastest pace
      not the best way to track, however. An hour,
it was raining, and by the time we returned
to the lean-to, it was blowing straight
down. Despite waterproof clothing, we were soaked
and shivering. Boleslav started a fire
in the rain and indicated that we should all sit
on the ground and eat. Instead, we rushed
to the lean-to. Crowded, standing, under
the lean-to, we broke out the cheese and bread.
Dimitar had brought deer meat salami
      and two other kinds of meat. The rain
worsened, so we ate all the bread, then exchanged
reports on wildlife signs. Sidar Rangelov,
the famous archer and tracker, who had said
he would meet us at the lean-to, had not shown.
He was either dry somewhere or had greeted
the wolves in the valley

When the rain let up, we crossed a ridge
and walked through a haggard forestry unit
downhill to a logging road. Only deer signs
were seen on this part of the ridge. Dimitar ran
to get the jeep, and we met him at the bottom
of the valley. Back at the hut, I walked over
to the river, then walked along the bank a way,
until I could get to the middle by hopping
across boulders. I meditated with moving
water. After an hour, I tossed twigs in the river
and watched where the current took
them—in one place the current flattened
them on the bottom. I looked for trout. I saw
a few shadows and knew
they were hiding, so I left them alone.

Teasing the Trackers

Dimitar and I got up early and went outside
to talk. First, he went to water a tree and I ambled
down to the river to wash in freezing water,
knowing his would not filter down for many hours.
Then we sat outside and talked while the rangers
slept. It was drizzling. I walked alone down
the road looking for signs. I heard a jeep;
it was young Dimitar, returning from Kazanluk—
he had seen fresh wolf tracks downhill.

    He raced uphill to get the others and I jogged
downhill. After ten minutes Georgiu caught up,
and ten minutes later, four tired rangers
arrived. We walked about four kilometers
without seeing anything but deer signs. Then,
        one wolf print—
it was over the tracks of the jeep,
so it was new! Then, another wolf print
on the other side of the road. Georgiu measured
them and I made notes and photographed
them. One average male wolf and one female
or yearling. Our numbers had turned uniqueness
into averages. The two walked down the road,
stopping where a roe deer had crossed, but
continuing downhill. After three kilometers,
we lost the tracks, but keep walking.
Then we backtracked to the last track
and looked for evidence of direction change.
We found a set of roe deer tracks leading off
the road. I wondered if the wolves had left
the road before then, but found no more tracks.

    No tracks up from the river
or down to it. Everyone got ahead of me so
I amused myself by tracking them, which was hard to do
on gravel. I caught up to Boleslav and Dimitar,
a botanist and an ornithologist, who took
pleasure in identifying birds and flowers
for me. And I joyed in learning them.
Suddenly the survey was over.

Following Wolves

Karakachans

At the Balkani Wildlife office in Pernik, the staff
and I crowded into a Daihatsu jeep and drove through
the ruined mine by the edge of the city to visit
the Karakachan sheep dog farm. They were noisy
in the dark; noisy and threatening—only
the puppies were friendly. Then we drove
to the village of Sadovik (Pop. 67), where Ivailo's family
had an ancient farmhouse. We were greeted
by a young sheepdog, noisy but friendly,
rejected by a shepherd for that very reason.

Petar and I each claimed a room upstairs
and the family of Ralitsa, Ivailo and their son
stays downstairs. Dinner was about ten; soup
and salad, with grilled worst. The village
was dark long before we went to warm sleeping bags.

Circling Sites

Breakfast was toast with organic blackberry
jam and water. We decided Vlado, Ralitsa, Petar
and I would do the survey. We drove north
for an hour to a small village, Staracelo, on a dead
end road. We parked in a field near an old
house, careful to display our binoculars
and talk about the birds—we had told
the villagers we were bird-watchers.

We walked up out of town. The forest
had been cut thirty years ago and replanted
in pine. The pine made ribbons around
the mountains, which were rocky and open
at the top, with grass and scrublands below.
Many old roads and trails. It had
rained, so prints abounded. Foxes had left their scat
on rocks and old bottles so that we could admire
their art. Wolves had left theirs along the roads
and at intersections, so we could read
the boundaries of their presence. Dogs and jackals

had left prints and dung anywhere.
It was a good area for mammals. I had become
expert at sighting scat, and worried that I might
overlook an actual live wolf.

*Vlado finds
a wolf print*

We made a giant circle until we saw all possible
trap sites. The road continued quite a way,
although it seemed only to be used
for a rare harvest. No real evidence
of herding. Along the way, we ate rosehips
and wild cranberries. Ralitsa collected beechnuts,
and I collected scat, running out of plastic bags
then using kleenex wrappers, and finally loading
the rubber pockets in my fishing vest. Back
to the jeep and back to the house, we ate bread
and apples until dinner was ready after Ten.

Crossing Borders

After yogurt and toast, we drove due west
towards the Yugoslav border and a range
of hills. This area had never been investigated.
Fewer tracks and scat than we expected. The walk
was long. And, every time we found scat,
     we found blackberries—
the connection had to be real—everyone,
including us humans, ate the berries and shit
three meters later. So, we cut large branches
of berries and ate them like popsicles
as we walked directly up the highest

local peak, about fourteen hundred meters.
We took our first and only break
of the two days, eating peanuts and cookies
    and looking at Yugoslavia or Bulgaria
in the blue distance. We walked back
to the village, and stopped in a cafe
for tea. The owner excitedly told us that he
had seen a wolf that very morning, following
us as we were going the other direction
out of town.   He was so frightened
that he had gone to a gypsy baba and had a spell
cast for him, to remove the curse
of the sighting. We sighed and ran outside
and followed the tracks on top of ours for a way,
one of us always looking backwards to make
sure we were not being followed again.
Complimenting the skill of the wolf at tracking,
we went back to the house for a snack of soup
and melons and discussed the treachery of wolves.

The Gypsy's Curse
Tracking wolves
    we traipsed the entire landscape
from village to river valley
        to mountains. Nothing.

Back at the village
    we stopped at a bar
and heard that the wolf
        had been tracking us.

The bartender saw the wolf following
    our trail five minutes behind us.
He was scared so badly he went
        to the gypsy to have the curse lifted.

He was lucky, all we saw was cranes
    and thousands of signs
but the gypsy could not take
        our blisters away.

In the Hide of the Wolf

In the mountains, we found a trail
between two villages, lined with sheep prints
    and manure. We saw a few cattle
on the hillside, but no sheep at all. No wolves,
    either. The trail led directly to the jeep,
where Grisha was waiting, eating his cheese
    sandwich. We got sandwiches too
and had a picnic, discussing the perversity
    of wolves. Later, we drove to a rendezvous
with the others.

        They were not there, so we drove
to another village where a man had killed a wolf
    last year. We asked to see the skin,
but he misunderstood and tried to sell
it to us. I finally agreed to buy it for twenty
dollars and one of our brochures.

It was smallish and not cured completely.
My friends assumed that I would put
it on the floor of my room, but
    I had another plan.

At the night blind the following week
at dusk, I walked to the hill above
    the drinking pond.
I lay down with the hide, by the broken
beech tree. Watching the hillside
    I pulled it over me and
got up on my hands and knees
and moved between trees.

What did I feel? Sense? Hunger? Prey? The smell
    was disturbing. No horses
approached. No pigs drank that night.
    And no wolves crossed my path.

I buried him below the floor of the blind
like an honored Mesopotamian lord.

Daylight Equals Death

I could not see the wolf
   at first
then the tan and brown shape
   resolved itself
on the pile of cut firewood—
only because of the curves.
I was told that the hunter got fifty Leva
and the pile of firewood for bringing
in the wolf, a young male,
foolish enough to travel
during the day and foolish enough
     to pause
before the hunter and his stick.
   I asked to have the wolf, but was denied.
The ears would be taken for proof
of the kill, the meat disposed of, and the pelt
given to the lucky hunter.

An unlucky young male wolf

Shadow Play
    Wolf folds
             shadows
around his shape to move unseen—
but the shadows remain
a few moments longer
                  for me to see.
The air adjusts slowly to absence.

A shadow plays
with its source   with the observer;
       the forest hides
the shadow, the air above the grass
anticipates its form—

Landscape with Horses
Moving slowly towards
the trees, eating a path
   up the hill so that by dark
they were hidden
      though no wolf
could fail to follow their smell.

Released for winter
to forage for themselves
   they covered the hill in front
of my night blind tree.

One was curious
perhaps remembering
      a gift from humans
but she drifted off.

It is simple ecology
to read the scents and relate
      them to others.
It is common
sense to eat and sleep
   with the herd.

Digging Badger

It was still raining, but very lightly. Vlado
and Galya dropped me and Grisha at another
village; we were going to walk to the village
of Vereda, where they would park and make
their own survey. We started up the river valley.
Grisha, the forester, had looked once
at the map and then given it back
to Vlado. I asked if he knew where we were going;
he said yes, he was good at maps.
Immediately going up from the river, I found
wolf tracks; two wolves, moving single file,
one large, one small, maybe a yearling.
The rain washed away almost everything
but these, so they had to be made this morning.
　　Some tracks were very good,
so I measured and photographed them. We followed
for over three kilometers, losing
them sometimes on rock, grass, or gravel,
but always finding them again.

Then we found a strange digging
and a badger print. The badger had been looking
for beetles. In one of the diggings, the badger
had left scat filled with beetle carapaces.
We backtracked the badger
since he was heading down hill, perhaps after

the wolves passed uphill. A few
stone marten tracks with five toes. Going
downhill, we heard a shout—it was Vlado
and Galya, who had just found the wolf tracks,
    where we were five minutes before.
Vlado took some measurements, but his seemed
larger than mine by a centimeter. We compared
notes; he was measuring from the claw tip
     and rounding down,
while I rounded up from the pads.

The four of us continued. The rain stopped
and the sun peeked out, so we stopped
and had lunch, a cheese sandwich and apple
each. We were sitting amid many caterpillars,
same color but different sizes. We noticed
bees, flies, spiders, and beetles, out now. Three different
kinds of flowers but none of us knew the Latin
names—mammalogists, huh. We discovered
    an old car pushed over a hill,
the first abandoned car I had seen here.
Sasha said they were repaired forever.

Two more ridges and we found the correct village
right away, but we were at the wrong end
of it and had to go up hill a few
kilometers. At the bar, we had beer and coke.

Wolf scat

Black Peak

The trip to the peak was uneventful, although
it was baking hot and Blake, a visting
volunteer, and I had to drink
from mountain streams every ten minutes,
as well as soak our heads. The views
were tremendous and the skies were clear.
Tired, I pushed my legs like wooden pistons.
We finally arrived after Four. At the top,
a stone marten ran from us around the building,
    one of the old radars domes
from the army installation. As we walked around
we startled the marten again, he continued clockwise
and hid. Two raptors were floating around,
a buzzard and eagle. After resting
for an hour and looking over the north
and south valleys, we started down.

The trip down was harder on the legs but easier
on the lungs. We got back just as the sun set.
At the hizha cafe, we ordered salads and chicken,
as well as tea, beers, and cokes. We had
to order from the bar, pay, and then give the order
to the cook, who cooked it and told the barmaid,
who told us when to pick up the food from
the kitchen. Alas, the cook was lazy and the barmaid
had to keep reminding him to cook the food.

Black Butterflies

The next day in the forest I hid the borrowed bicycle
in the leaves and walked along the other trail past
the hunting hut, to another water
catchment. I walked up hill and down
looking for trails and wolf signs. Found
some interesting looking scat
but could not decide if it was
wolf or fox—it looked too small
to be a wolf. I lay down on
a bed of leaves and watched
a hollow for movement. Many

birds, no animals. On the way
back, I noticed that on every bit
of scat on the road, mostly cow
or horse, were two black
butterflies that lifted when I walked by
and then alighted after I passed. Another
day without a wolf sighting.

Black Woodpecker Playing Tag

On Sunday in the afternoon, I went alone
on a walk to the north ridge. Tracked a wolf
then a fox. Counted many roe deer
prints crossing the road.
Mouse prints in the snow
by the side. This road went up through
the hills towards a state microwave
tower.   At a small settlement
of houses, I stopped to talk to a man working
on his car. The weather was beautiful
and sunny. I wanted to talk about wildlife,
but he wanted to know where I was going.
Bird watching, I said. Going back, I played tag
with a black woodpecker.

Climbing

The first road was level and wide. After calculating
exactly which ridge we should climb, we left
the road and climbed straight up. After an hour
of hard climbing, we crossed an old road, used
it to go higher, then straight up again, going past
a small meadow, through more beech forest
    to a high meadow—
almost every ridge had a natural meadow on top,
where sheep used to graze—they still are natural,
in the sense they were created by thousands
of years of human use and many species had adapted
to them, but now only deer and wild pigs grazed there—
the diversity of species that had slowly emerged was being
gradually lost now that juniper shrubs and trees

had started to reclaim it, an unusual situation.
    I got to the field first and looked around
for the prune tree that the bear had torn apart
the year before. Not finding it, I cruised
the meadow, finding a large pond, filled
with wild pig tracks, a few frogs and many
new tadpoles. No bear or wolf signs.
After a rest in the sunny field, we inspected
the perimeter and the spruce plantations
to the west. We lay down to nap
in the sun, a new habit I appreciated.

Reluctant to leave, we walked slowly
down the next eastern ridge, towards the reservoir
for the power station. After a few kilometers,
the ridge turned straight down and we plunged
through the dark cool forest looking for a trail. Many
animals paths but no trails. Then we found
an old wolf scat; the measurements were perfect,
but it was old and white. Most organic material
had leached out in the rains. Only hairs
with a few small bones were left.

Further down the slope, fresh bear scat,
filled with seeds and rosehips. But, no other signs.
Good habitat for bear, but we did not see a likely
den in that area. We found many kinds of orchids,
but were unable to find a path.
    Among the rocks, an opening. We hauled
our bodies up the face. With Blake
on guard, I entered the den and lay
near the entrance on a pile of fine
grasses. I might have stayed,
but it wasn't mine
and I did not want to leave
too much scent behind. I clambored
down headfirst. We edged
our way to the steep ravine.

Bear den

The razor back ridge
had been going down much longer
than it went up. Finally
we crossed a path
that led to the eastern branch
of the Vidima river, so we followed
the river back to the Vets water station.

Night Wolves

Green Shapes

I started hiking before One o-clock, reaching
the first landmark, Hizha Pleven, on the first ridge.
Over a coke, I asked the host to point out
the trail to Mandrata. He did, and said to follow
the yellow poles, and it should take only
two hours to get there. Knowing it got dark
    at 6:24, I set a good pace. After half
an hour I lost the poles. So, I decided to cut directly
into the beech forest over the ridge. After
an hour I admitted that might have been a mistake,
no trail met my feet. Then I tried to head
south to where the trail should be. Another
hour passed and still no trail. But I crossed
    a stream and was heading up the next
ridge. Definitely lost, I looked at the map, and saw
where I had missed the trail. Rather than back
track, I kept going straight to the next ridge.

After another hour, I could see
the next landmark, the cheese factory,
with binoculars. At this point I went due south
up the ridge to try to intersect the trail,
which should be heading towards me. After
a while I found a wildlife trail and followed
it. Old horse manure marked it so
I knew someone had been here. The trail
led through the deep beech woods and up
past another ridge.
    Finally near the top
of the fourth ridge, I saw the roof
of a spring that I recognized. I climbed
up and got water. The sun had set but it was still
light enough to walk. The trail led to Mandrata,
the cheese factory and then over a hill to the night
blind overlooking a game trail and watering hole.

In the last of the light, I arranged the sleeping
bag, the matches and viewing equipment.

Spent all night watching the water
hole with the Russian night scope. At first,
the sky kept getting darker and darker. No animals.
Then the moon came up. Then the owl started
hooing and making other sounds. Then another
night bird started calling. Over the night, an elk
came by and bellowed, announcing mating
season, then a wild pig grunted up slope.
A ground squirrel ran up to the chakalo,
illuminated by the night scope, which
I finally got focused and working. Half
an hour later I saw a green shape divide the field—
    it moved like a wolf—the first sighting!
But I could not tell for sure until I measured the prints.
Then nothing for an hour. I dreamed.
About Five I got in the sleeping bag to keep
warm and slept for an hour.

In the light I walked down to the watering
hole and counted footprints, about ten surni
(roe deer), one elen (elk), two wild swine,
and about nine horses, which I had seen
the evening before on their way to a quieter
pasture for the night,
    and one new set of wolf prints
that did not even veer towards the water.
     I swept the leaves and dirt
out of the chakalo and fitted an old table cloth
over a hole in the wall. I hung the candles
and matches from a nail and left. Then, I tried
to find the real trail and did
    immediately—it had been
around the entire time but it skirted
the ridges. So I walked back and it only took
two hours. At the Hizha I had another
coke and went down the trail to the water
plant. On the way, I met Andrei, Bulchru,
and Dimitar, repairing the fence along
the steep trail. We exchanged stories
and I went on my way back to Aprilci.

Brown Bear Prints

At 2:30 I walked to Vidima and then
to Mandrata, which took almost
five hours. Made notes and photographs
on the way. I was in snow now,
but it was rotten and made walking
hard. The road curved west
and I looked ahead—

(Version One: Human Perception)
Looking for tracks in the snow
Walking around the corner
    Head down
        Movement
    Recognition
Human shape
Raise a hand in greeting
Raise a voice in greeting
        No answer
Dignified retreat up the hill
    Not human
Bearness?
Cubness?
    Danger?
Walked slowly towards them

(Version Two: Calculated Observation)
Looking for tracks in the snow
Head down
Walking up the ten percent grade
Through the pine forest
Observing the movement
    Stopped
           Ursus arctos horribilis
Good specimen, close,
      Started observing
She observed in return
before pushing the cub uphill
And following herself.
    Stopped
Looked back assessing danger.

Dropped
my pack, pulled
out the gear for measuring.
Got to the tracks and measured,
recording the wind, weather
    snow, location
Then measured the tracks,
Estimated weight, calculated gait
Continued looking uphill
      Backtracked downhill
Looking for scat
To see what they ate

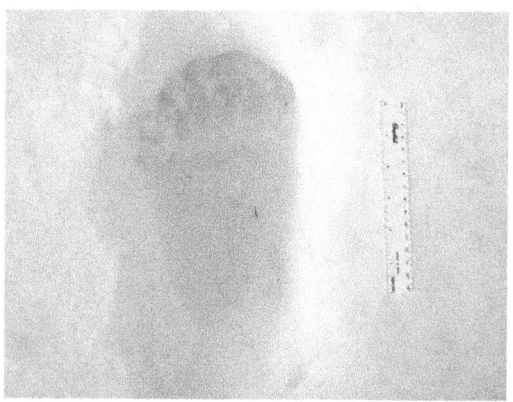

Bear track

(Version Three: Ursine Cognition)
Presence, yes,
  Danger, no
    Bear, no
      Other, yes
Move, yes
  Push cub uphill
    Stop, assess
Bear-like other
  Danger possible
    Intent unknown
      Attack, no
        Continue direction

(Version Four: Human Narrative)

Turning the corner
I saw a large man with a dog in the road.
I hailed them and they moved off
the road up hill into the trees without
a word. Then I realized I had seen a brown
bear with her cub. After a moment of indecision,
tempered with fear, I walked to look
at the tracks, singing softly praises
to all the souls of the forest—bear tracks
leading uphill —these were brown bears, like
American Grizzlies. I measured one
track, about the size of my foot
    but wider. I paused and looked
into the darkening forest.

I walked around the curve and realized
that it would intersect the upward path
of the bear. But I kept walking. The snow
was unbroken again. As I walked
up I entered a cloud, then a series of dark
pine forests. I was getting nervous, and then
I found a wolf track coming towards me—
that meant he turned off the trail when
he heard me coming. I suspected the bear
did too. Maybe they were both waiting
to eat me; maybe they would fight it out
to see who got to feed on me, the tasty
potato-filled clod. Then I came out
of the forest and saw four concrete walls
without a roof. it might work as shelter
but I decided to press on to
the night blind. In the snow, I lost the road
but keep going up. Through one last impenetrable
woods and I was on the ridge.

It was all white
and I could not find the trail, but I could see
the trees by the blind.
I walked out of the cloud

under a half moon. The mountains were cloaked
in higher clouds, the valleys in lower clouds. Only
this ridge was free. It was quite beautiful
and I was quite relieved. Now I could see death
coming! As I walked along I saw another
wolf track that I was backtracking. Then,
I realized again that the wolf and I should have passed
each other on the way. I stared into the shadows
at what could have been the eye and face of a wolf.

Night view towards the night blind

I went downhill and past the water
hole, reached the blind and made myself
at home, eating a few peanuts and drinking
some water. I sat for an hour and observed
but no one was presenting herself. I took a nap
but had muscle cramps, so went back to observing.
The moon was so bright I could use regular
binoculars. Back to sleep, but had more
cramps. So, just observed. I saw a shape move.
The ground squirrel. Then the owl in the tree.
A larger shape—a pig, I was not sure.
Getting in the sleeping bag on the floor with

my wrapped ski pants for a pillow, I slept
a little. I woke to footsteps in the snow outside
but it was a Karakachan horse
left loose for the winter.

At dawn, I cleaned the window,
stuffed the pack, and left. It was bright enough,
so I started back down. On the way
I measured the footprints again, and found
new ones either crossing my trail or following
it. The last was a bear that had followed
my prints for several hundred meters
before turning down slope, perhaps when
she heard me coming, now. The snow was frozen
and easier to walk on. I walked all the way
to Aprilci. The trip took five hours. My legs
were sore so I took a shower with everything
on, clothes, boots, snow, mud, and rocks.
Then I recorded the notes and measurements.

Freezing

While Angel went to the bazaar, I worked
in the windowless, heatless, furnitureless office,
the old storage room above the barber shop
and soda magazine that I rented for ten
Leva a month—a good deal despite its many
shortcomings. I zipped my coat up and put
more cardboard under my feet. I had to finish
the wolf survey results and ship them off
to Dimitar, then finish the observation log
for the year and send it to Georgiu. So I worked
until noon. Angel returned with kebabche, so we had
them with leftover mashed potatoes. After more
computer work, I walked to the Black Peak
to complete another set of observations. For dinner
I fixed a pizza to celebrate another week
of not being eaten by wolves and bears.
The evening was spent in the joy of touching
Angel and the joy of being connected.

Wild Horses

By the time we got to Sadovik it was past
ten. It was raining. A dog barked threateningly—
it was the two-year old Karakachan named
Arul. I tried to make friends but he rammed
his nose into my thighs and snorted
and sniffed. We seemed to be friends now
although I did not return the affection.
Vlado decided that we should have rice.
I cut bread. Grisha made soup. By midnight,
we had finished and gone to bed. Vlado slept by
the wood fire; the rest of us went
upstairs, with its three small hard beds.

It was raining. We made breakfast of yogurt,
cereal and leftovers, then forged out
with our rain gear. As we were driving to a new
group of villages to investigate
for wolf presence. Ralitsa called and asked
us to help round up some Karakachan horses,
which had been left out to pasture for eleven
years—seriously, the owner turned them
out and now, three generations later,
he wanted to round them up. If we helped,
we could have a few. But, we heard they had divided
into three separate herds, lead by two males
and a female. At the assigned location, we found
no evidence of horses. Vlado asked
a few shepherds, while I walked through the river
looking for prints or scat—nothing. After
a few more calls, we gave up and drove
on to the first village, Kovachentsi.

Lost Between Villages

Grisha dropped off the three of us then drove
to the rendezvous village, which was two hills
away; he planned to make a circle on foot then meet
us about Three. We walked up through
the village talking to the shepherds
and farmers. This area had been inhabited
for many thousands of years. Vlado told me
twenty years before, hundreds of thousands
of sheep and cattle filled the area
but now both the human and animal
      populations were dwindling.
Those left were self-sufficient, but could not sell
their animal products, such as milk and meat,
because they could not meet the new European
standards. One shepherd usually gathered sheep
and goats from fifteen or twenty families
and then took them into the hills for the day,
returning each to the proper owner before dusk.
The fields for potatoes and other crops
were being planted now; they were usually
on the edges of the villages, although each house
had a small garden. Many people, mostly women,
were out working these fields, planting the spring
crops. We saw very few young people.

Then we were out of the village and the fields
and into a small scrub forest. We heard

then saw a cuckoo, then a raven, then a harrier.
I found the first scat of the day, from a fox,
so naturally I measured and photographed
it, as if it were the only thing I might find. Then
we came across roe deer prints leading
up the hill from the river. Then shortly
afterwards the prints of a wolf who seemed
to be following but not chasing the deer—
the prints were of a small male or large female,
    although at this time of year
the females were pregnant. The rain was making
it hard to track because it is washing the prints away
as we followed, but we followed the wolf
for a kilometer or so uphill. The wolf was following
the road. I took photographs in the rain, surprised
that the camera still worked.   I was soaked
to the skin. On the other side of the road I found
a stone marten track, just one. Vlado and I discussed
why he would be out in a clearing and not
in the trees. Unlike pine martens, stone martens
had adapted to open areas and hunted mice.

Finally we descended into a village, but asked
and found out it was the wrong village!
A shepherd said, no, we must cross another
ridge. Then Vlado asked each shepherd
we passed and each gave slightly different
instructions. Finally, we reached the village,
but it was deserted. I smelled smoke, so Vlado
shouted. His shout was answered but it took
us a while to find the house. It turned out
that we had taken a wrong turn and should
have gone over another ridge. We walked
along a paved road which we were told
led to the village. At a major intersection, relatively
speaking since most roads were single
lane and the paving had worn through to gravel,
we saw a jeep drive by in the rain and shouted.
    It was Grisha, who figured we were lost
and got a shepherd to help him. The shepherd
talked with us for a while in the downpouring rain

then he walked back to his sheep and we drove on.

Another breakfast of yogurt and leftovers.
We drove to Svetlya and met Ralitsa. We decided
to divide up into three groups now and all meet
in Vereda, where we met yesterday. Now
we were checking the east ridges rather than
the west ridges. The trails were all grassy,
so we did not expect many tracks. Ralitsa, Grisha
and I dropped off Galya and Vlado, then dropped
off the car. We planned to make three large loops
around the village. After a while Grisha circled
south and Ralitsa and I continued up hill. We saw
a few summer houses near the top,
closed for the season. We saw another
cuckoo and a woodpecker, but no
    prints of any kind for a long time, then a fox
and a marten. The fox had been eating rosehips
for every meal, so the scat was yellow or pure red.
Some was displayed on rocks. The marten had left
scat on rocks for us to find, also, but it looked
like he had been eating meat, mice perhaps,
but no bones. Then we found several
wolf scats, which we collected and recorded
on the new forms. Several wolf prints, but
the rain had been unkind. We got lost
in a thorn forest, painful, then we came out
at a rock outcropping. I suggested
going straight down to the river. Ralitsa agreed,
but I found in hindsight that we would have had
an easier time going up the ridge and then
down through a meadow. For all its noise
and speed, the river was only two feet wide.

We drove back. Still no Vlado, so we napped
in the new sun. Finally he came up the hill,
led by the dog Arul. We compared notes,
and looked for a cafe but none were open,
so we drove back to the cold house in Sadovik.

Sofia Bus station

Ralitsa left for Pernik. We cleaned up, finished
the leftovers, and followed. To get
to the train, we had to have coffee again
and play musical cars. Ivailo was going
to Sofia, but had to wait for his brother. We talked
and waited. Ralitsa and Galya went on errands.
Finally, Simeon came and he, Ivailo, Grisha,
Vlado, and I drove to Sofia. We were dropped
off at the south bus station. Vlado took one bus,
Grisha and I got another and went to the city
center. From there I walked to the Hotel Maya
and got a room, which looked across
the boulevard at the statue of liberty
and wisdom—she had an owl and a book.
Everything was lit up, but the room was quiet.
    I worked on the color brochure, then got ready
to take the pieces to the printer in Lovich.

Caged Wolf

Krasimir asked me if I wanted to walk around
while I was waiting for the wolf brochure.
I said I thought I would walk to the zoo, but then
he got his coat and followed—apparently,
he meant with him. So, we walked to the zoo
in Lovich, the second largest in Bulgaria.
The parking lot was empty, although
    four teenagers loitering around
the entrance. The inspector waved
us through the gates, then stopped us to say
that there was not enough money for food
for the animals. The zoo looked abandoned;
some of the cages were broken; everything
was overgrown with grass, weeds and trees.
First, we walked to the bird cages and saw
eagles and hawks. The insides of the cages
were clean and the birds looked healthy.

Many of the animals were missing, no giraffe
no elephant; others, a brown bear, monkeys,
seemed to be inside.
    I sought the wolf cage;
the wolf was lying on a rock outcropping built
over the stone den. He walked down and came
directly to the fence. I put my fingers through
and he rubbed against them, then continued
the length of the cage rubbing on the wires.
I looked in his eyes, but only saw resignation.
I wondered if any wildness was left; maybe
    if he were suddenly free. He was shorter
and stockier than the Siberian wolves,
but then he was a different subspecies.
His winter coat was very brown, a little
like Legend, my wolf-friend left in Oregon.
He walked back up and flopped down again.
I wondered if wolves had names; no, names
would not be necessary, some patterns
were more unique than names.
    I sighed and walked downhill. We visited
the leopard, polar bear, red deer, and surni.

One large American bison, some ducks,
an otter, three fox, and many more deer. The gong
announced that the zoo would close in half
an hour, so we walked to the exit and paid.
We had been the only people there.

Speaking for Wolves
We walked to see the Minister
of the Environment. Through the locked bronze
doors, we told the guards we had an appointment.
The Minister came down the wide spiral stairs
to meet us and we paraded back up to a large
meeting room. He was an elderly man
with a doctorate in forest engineering.
He was confused as to why we were meeting,
he said they had an inventory
of wolves since 1997 and good knowledge
of them long before that.

I praised the country's efforts
and suggested that it could become
the first nation to create a complete
inventory of its resources, and have
a science-based monitoring
for wolves. But, he replied
there was no money, and that was that.

I suggested that his knowledge was gained
by hunters looking out the windows
of hizhas and counting dollar-green shadows.
He asked what we would do. Ralitsa described
our surveys, that took us into the depths
of the forests. He politely asked
us to send him reports. He smiled a lot,
but his body language indicated he
was helpless, even if he thought
it would be a good idea. We exchanged
pleasantries about the weather
and thanked him for his time, the only thing
he had to give. Afterwards, we stopped

for tea at the Central Market, and talked
about sending reports, or nothing.

We stopped at the Pernik yard where
Filip and Ivailo had been making
traps for stone martens, so we inspected the traps,
played with them. Ralitsa left to buy groceries,
especially cheeses and breads. She bought
food for the dog, Arul, two dozen chicken heads.
Finally, about Eight we arrived at the house
in Sadovik. Arul was waiting happily.
    Angel cooked omelets and I made cheese
sandwiches. After eating, we played with the new
GPS devices and walky talkies. We talked for a few
hours about the project and went to sleep.

Arul Mountain

We drove to the base of Arul mountain
and divided into two teams. Sabas decided
that Angel and I were too slow,
    so he left alone.
Angel and I went with Petar, who drove
to another town two ridges away. After hiking
uphill for three hours, we met Sabas on
a ridge; he was loafing in the sunny grass.
We ate our cheese sandwiches and fingered
over the maps. There did no seem to be any
wolf signs in the area. We saw hawks, buzzards,
and frogs, then signs of roe deer and fox.

We split up again and circled around
the ridge. We get lost, although the GPS unit
told us where we needed to go. Not finding
a trail we crossed a rock ridge and talus slope,
finally following a stream to a trail. We had
seen the village two ridges away, but once
in the forest got lost again and off the trail.
I took a few photographs, then sat on a downed
tree and made notes about the signs we did
notice.   Not a single wolf sign, though.

Sabas boils the traps

Back at the jeep, Sabas was waiting. We drove
back to the village of Sadovik by mid-afternoon.
It was time to prepare the traps by boiling them
with willow shoots; these were the traps made
here from the Romanian model of a trap
sold in Texas—we only had to pay for materials.
Sabas lit started the fire. The clothes, stakes,
chains, and bags were also
boiled. I went to the house to start
boiling our food, pasta.

After a breakfast of leftovers
and cereal, we made sandwiches for lunch
and drove to Paramunska mountain,
a new area where we had heard that a wolf
print was found the week before. As one
group, we walked out of another small
village; perhaps twenty people
lived there. On the trail, we saw more
deer and fox signs, as well as squirrel and hare
prints. We walked from rocky barrens to
young trees, then an old beech forest. The wood
seemed to be harvested by the coppice
method. Only posts or rails had been cut.

After Two, we were back at the vehicle, and drove
to Breznik for soup and salad. Then
we drove to Pernik and dropped off
the jeep at a parking lot near an abandoned
factory. This was necessary because the car
had been kidnapped twice for ransom
(and it had been paid twice).
    Then we walked to a bus stop
and waited for a bus to Sofia. We took the bus,
which let us off at the western bus station.
Then we had a take a tram to the city center.
Sabas went with us, since he had to catch
another bus to his apartment. It started
raining and we got soaked. We went back
to the Hotel Maya and checked in. I thought
we were again the only people in the hotel,
so we had our choice of rooms. We ate
a sandwich at the Irish Harp bar.

Embracing Metal
We both knew, he and I,
        that it would never be used
                that I would not trick him
        into stepping into that embrace

We had a metalworker forge the traps
        in Pernik, from a Texas design
but with extra rubber on the bite
        I tested it with my arm—oww!

We boiled the traps, chains, gloves
                bags, and our clothes
        in a tub with willow shoots
We dried them on trees.

We carried the bags through the village
showing our binoculars to people
who thought we were bird watchers.
        At the remote trail, we marked

certain trees. Made a hole at the base
and carefully covered the set trap
with leaves and ground wolf shit.
Then, on the bark, sprayed a fish scent
of remarkable potency.

We left and slept well. The next day
quietly walked along the trail
noting the perfect undisturbed traps.
Sighed quietly all the way back.

Day after day, twice a day, in rain
     and sun, we walked.
I started smiling. My ten years
of tracking was not enough to overcome
their heritage of four thousand years
     of outwitting hunters.
Every day was a hike in the forest
a chance to see other things: migrations of
salamanders, evenly spaced every
ninety-four meters,
     phalanxes of butterflies resting
on grandmother's soul, the bones
of a wild pig, unlucky or slow,
every bit of flesh gone, except a
skirt around an ankle, and up the hill
a pile of wolf shit every nine meters.
Silent hello to you, too, clever friends.

*Salamandrica
heads to water*

Old Karl Marx contended that we live in cages,
part natural, part made; human action

could modify them. Still, it is being trapped.
Humans invented traps to catch
animals. The animal got a treat, but had trouble
escaping from the table, so to speak,
a short-term gain followed by a long-term cost,
usually unwanted and inescapable.
    We are trapped in a cycle
Of consumption. I write this with my light
pen on a waterproof tablet. Self-actualization
is postponed for self-gratification. That
is one trap. Energy another. We get caught in
others, technological traps like waste
dumps, cultural ones
   like agriculture, which gave us beer
and concentrated food, and personal
traps, such as smoking and tasting chocolate.

Making Lines

At Pernik it was raining and I had to wait
another hour for the bus to Sadovik. I bought
the ticket and asked for the correct sector
and the clerk said right in front. The bus wandered
the roads through Breznik and another twelve
villages before getting there. One of the last
three on the bus, I walked up the hill
to the other side of the village.
    At the house I was greeted
by Arul and another Karakachan
who barked wildly, until I presented my hands
to be smelled. The new dog was one
of the puppies I had seen in September,
a young female called Shara.   Ralitsa was
with a Belgian, Carleigh, a photographer who
had been volunteering for the past five
years. Vlado and Sabas were back
from ten days camping in the far west; their trap
line had caught only a small boar so they
had pulled the traps today. We talked about
the problems, equipment, and strategies.
Ralitsa would check the traps tomorrow

and Vlado and I would scout new territories.
So, we drank and talked until dark.

Guns and Laws

Vlado and I left, walking to the village
of Izbor and the high ridge
beyond. We walked over the ridge, Mogilla
Hill into the forestry unit, and to Rekalska,
the hill next to the river. We found
weasel, ermine, and marten
scat. Then fox prints and scat. We saw
a wild cat ducking in front of a bush.
Vlado identified the birds, including
        the bee-eater.
We ended up on a small paved
road leading to a forest unit.
From the garden next
to the concrete hut, a civil wretch
told us his boss was in the woods waiting
to shoot us without warning. Vlado nodded
but reminded him that was illegal,
and we left with bad feelings.
    Vlado was pissed, quietly furious.
As we walked, he guessed
they had some illegal operation
and rehearsed all the laws
in Bulgaria relating to guns. I was more
worried about being shot for a wolf,
then Vlado said that trespassers
had to be warned before a shooting,
furthermore, the person with the fewest
weapons was presumed innocent, so,
if we had a revolver and the forester had a rifle,
we would be innocent. He had a cell phone
and I had my Swiss army knife.

We walked around the ridge without incident.
It started to rain. Finally, we came to a road
but veered off it and over another ridge
to Sadovik, returning in time for a late

lunch. That afternoon, we discussed
the strategy for the next few days. Ralitsa
left for Pernik. The house ran out
of water, so we had to go to the well
to get buckets and fill old plastic bottles.
I was wet and freezing, so I changed clothes,
crawled into the sleeping bag
and read for an hour. Then, I started
     to make dinner, although
I was not interested in cooking or eating.
     Macaroni with a tomato sauce,
with onion, mushroom, and some
meatballs. We talked until dark, then
Vlado and Sabas went to the local pub
for a few drinks and to see if a waitress
had developed a crush on one of them
(I was considered too old, but age lets me
avoid the unwanted attentions of young men).

Lyalitsa Hill trap line

Empty Traps
Vlado, Sabas and I got up early
    and drove to Lyalitsa to check
traps. Sabas dropped us off and drove
to Paramoon. We walked straight
up the ridge and found an old trail.
    I could not see where the traps
were. It started to rain. I finally noticed
        a spot of dead grass
and Vlado said that in fact each dead spot
covered a trap; fish fertilizer had been sprayed
on the trees. The mist played with us
around the peaks. It was a beautiful place
that shepherds no longer used. No
tracks or signs of wolf presence.
Fox scat, and many birds, but no other
mammals. All of the traps were undisturbed.
So, we walked back and waited
on the road for Sabas.

Sabas called on the new walky-talky
to say that his traps were also empty,
so we waited until he walked to
the jeep. He picked us up and we sat
in silence   these traps had to be checked
twice a day   rode back to the house
for a late breakfast of bread and eggs, with
left-over spaghetti and salami.
Vlado and I took the dogs
and walked out to the western part of town,
up into the hills, to look for wolf signs.
This an area frequently used by shepherds
for sheep and cattle
        hosted their evidence. We saw evidence
of weasels, but little else. The dogs
were wild, running back and forth. Back
at the house, we had butter sandwiches for dinner
and talked. Vlado walked to the pub alone.

More Empty Traps

Up early again, we were preparing to check
the traps, when Ralitsa called and asked us
to wait for her. Vlado went back
    into his sleeping bag
and I played with the dogs. Then Ralitsa
showed up and we all drove
to Lyalitsa, where Vlado and I pulled the first
set of traps.   Then we drive to Paramoon,
where Ralitsa and I walked out to pull the next
set. But, on the way, I spotted a few wolf prints,
new prints, made since the last rain the night
before. We carefully tracked the prints,
    but lost them in the forest a few
hundred meters from the traps.

Ralitsa moved first and motioned me to
stay but I pretended not to understand. We checked
all the traps along a path up the ridge into
the deep woods—this was where wolf prints
had been found a month ago by a forester. All
the traps were empty   we decided not
to pull them yet. We walked back, talking
about the new prints. Ralitsa drove back to Pernik
while Vlado and I make a lunch of cheese sandwiches,
then drove to Celo Sigurci, where we followed
the trail we took a month earlier, when I had found
two wolf trails leading over the ridge.
This time however, we walked for four hours
and found no traces, although the badgers,
fox, and martens were all at home, out of sight.
    We walked back to the jeep and drove
to Paramoon, where we hiked out to the last
set of traps we had checked that morning
and renewed the fish scent.

We got back to the house
and had cheese sandwiches, which I liked
and rarely tired of. Vlado forced
me at knifepoint to go to the pub. We sat
with the old men from the village, playing

cards for toothpicks
although a few were toothless
and others sported steel teeth. We talked
about the soccer team. I had vodka
and Vlado a few beers. They asked who I was.
  Before I could answer, Vlado introduced me
as a bird-watcher from Canada. This explained
our strange crepuscular habits to the villagers,
and also guaranteed that they would not
        follow us and take the traps.

Always Empty Traps

Up at Five again, and out directly to check
the last string of traps, nine in a row uphill
from the village of Paramoon on Paramoon
mountain. We expected to catch a wolf, after
the manifest evidence yesterday and we had
renewed the scents. But, trap after trap,
    each withholding its conclusion
        nothing had disturbed our smooth lines.
We walked back slowly,
reviewing the trap placement
and any possible oversights. Back at the house,
we had a late breakfast of tea and toast.
I washed my clothes in a bucket—
it had been raining
for the past ten days and   everything was muddy.
The sun came out and things looked like they
might dry. Vlado took the dogs for a walk.

When he came back I fixed our staple,
cheese sandwiches, for lunch. Then
        we hiked west of Sadovik
again, through the hills that have been grazed
for thousands of years. These hills had not
grown back deep forests although a few
trees could serve as shelter for wolves.
We thought the sheep might be tempting,
especially since the populations of red deer
had been falling and now the roe deer

numbers were falling. We guessed
that poachers hunting at night with jeeps,
spotlights, and automatic weapons
had reduced the numbers. But, no
      wolf signs marked the area.
We are depressed and returned.
Vlado cried, 'not cheese again.' I shrugged,
must be the hungry old Thracian blood.
Vlado found an old chicken leg in the freezer.
I found some rice that I had bought in April.
Three cooked potatoes from Monday.
The rice was put in water at the bottom
   of a pan; the leg was sliced and added,
    then the potato pieces were layered
    on top and the mess was doused
    with olive oil and spices and cooked for an hour.
Vlado made a tomato salad, also, with sirene
cheese. He served dinner   quite decent.
His mood improved. We inspected the eighteen
maps of the region and discussed our strategy.
    Then we made another trip to the pub.
This time he had vodka and I smoked,
blowing smoke rings and French-inhaling
    until I was dizzy.
After another vodka I walked back
in the dark. Vlado stayed and talked with some
of the villagers—the people we saw working
in the fields as we were driving to trap areas.

*Vlado sets
a wolf trap*

Last Chance
Sunday
Last day
for the traps,
a third drizzling cloud
    masking high scrub trees
Wolf heads up
    dissolving into fog
      pausing close to the traps
        then staying the trail

Self-appointed guardian of wolves
    must move before
noting the disturbed needles
    dissolving in the fog

Around the curve of trails
    the two foggy peaks
We might as well pound drums
    before our steps
Vlado has a Russian wool hat, white.
    I count butterflies.

But we have packs with the blowguns,
    anesthetic, collars, knives, bandages.
Walk back to Paramoon
then walk up the mountain.
Halfway I remember that I forgot
    the blowpipe. Then we see
a roe deer, female, walking away from us.
A hundred meters later another roe deer.
Raven spots us and alerts the entire forest.
We hope the raven is teasing
    a trapped wolf.
The first trap is empty, then they all are.

Vlado sighs. I close my eyes
    Take alternate
traps. I spring mine, then wrap the chain
around it and drop it into an orange

bag. We drag
them all back down and got into the jeep. Another
sigh and we are gone. It is a beautiful sunny
morning, now, no rain or fog.

The wolves have been silent;
four thousand years
of being hunted has encouraged
	them to live at night
and not be tempted
by the scent of fish out of place.

Invited to extinction as guests of
communist hunting clubs, they
are allowed by indifference
back to the forests of the Balkans
then to Italy, Spain and France
Romania and Serbia
	sneaking under the radar.

Yulalona last on the red road

Counting Wolves

Back at the house we cleaned
and packed. By eleven,
we were in Pernik meeting
with Ralitsa and trying
to figure what was so problematic.
    We scanned sheets of data.
We finally concluded that wolf numbers
had in fact dropped over two years.
I suggest other areas
    around Smolyan, but that
was too far to commute, twice a day.
    And five years investment
here in Kraishde.

Vlado and Ralitsa decided to set out
        more of the traps in six days.
We looked at the budget
    it was easy to see the limits.
    Then Vlado and I walked to the bus stop
with our heavy packs. We saw the bus
in the distance and sprinted
the last half mile, making it easily,
although I was bellowing air.
        The bus went to Sofia. Vlado got
off at the city limit and I took
    the tramvai to the center.

*Arul waits
at the farm*

Lost in the Wild

Prelude to Dying
After several hundred yards the trail
disappeared in the stream   By following
the map I figured that I would go uphill
and parallel the stream   The rise
seemed ninety degrees and it took
me an hour to reach the ridge
after resting to catch my breath
        every tenth step
I followed an old landslide but used
the trees and shrubs for handholds
I questioned my lungs and they questioned
my age   No answers

From the ridge it got easier for a few
hundred yards but the ridge went straight
up the mountain Each time I thought
    I was near the top another
new ridge started   Then it started
to rain   I was not wearing raingear but
a shirt and a fishing vest   I got wet
My legs became leaden and hot
After the fifth sequence of rough climbing
I stopped on a small grassy knoll fifty
meters wide   I lay down on a hummock
of grass in the drizzle   With my heavy
backpack under my head I started to doze
    thinking that I might die if I had
to climb for another hour   This seemed like
a good place to die   the rain cooled me
and the breeze was light   Sounds
only of birds   I felt at peace   I watched clouds
felt the rain and again thought dying
here might not be so bad   I dozed some more
then struggled awake   Judging by
the wetness of my coat I had rested
for twenty minutes   I realized that if
I could not make it by sundown
I would have to find a place to sleep

So I rolled over   The first five steps
were slightly downhill   refreshed I started
climbing again

　　The next ridge had a sheer
rock face   It was easier than the landslide
or grass but I thought that I could not turn
back because handholds were so difficult
My pack unbalanced me   I started to fall
but grabbed an old pine limb with splinters
and the force of my grip tore off my watch
and broke it—the second since February
I noticed some very good caves just the right
size for bears   I peaked into one but saw no
evidence it was lived in—how could the bear
　　reach it?   But then why not?
The top of the ridge became a needle
so I had to climb along the side grateful
for the few small pines   I swung from pine
to pine like a northern-jungle Tarzan   grateful
for my a careful attention to those
novels   I thought each ridge was the peak
because I could see light behind
the pines   but I was fooled each time

Then after two more overwhelmingly steep
and sharp ridges I finally reached the top
which was a rocky mountain meadow
It was the highest peak around so I could see
the valley and lower peaks   No evidence
of a path or hut   I started to walk along the sides
but the grasses and junipers were tall
I moved upslope again   It was still raining
I was soaked to the waist and getting wetter
only my rain hat kept my shoulders dry
　　I walked down a little to look for shelter
I had been climbing for over six hours
Then I saw a break in the rock wall and looked
for a rock overhang   In the near distance I saw
what looked like a path so I climbed down
through the junipers   I spotted the small painted

bars that marked a park trail I jumped
down relieved   I turned east knowing that
the hut had to be somewhere but knowing
that if I was wrong I would have to walk
hours to the western hut   The trail
was fairly comfortable although it followed
the ridges   After fifty minutes I turned a corner
    and saw a three-story hut made
of stone just below a peak

Tri-Color Paths

I stayed for two days eating mushrooms
and water   Then I started down the mountain
following the recommended trail indicated
    by blue white and green bars
painted on rocks ever ten meters   The first hour
was through the beech forest then the trail
dove directly downhill through some pines
I heard a fox bark as I passed a hollow I barked
back   after a hundred meters he barked again
Then nothing but birds   It took only another
hour to get to lowest mountain hut then
another hour to reach the bus at the Chiflik basin
    The forest was the beautiful solid beech
of the small reserve Kazya Stena   At the bus
stop I had a coke and waited for forty minutes

Howling

Today I biked to Severen Djendem near
the water station at the foot of the Pleven
ridge   Met Bulchru and Dimitar on the way
they were cutting firewood from the trees
near the road   We talked then I continued
After leaving my bike at the water station
     I walked up the hill past
the hut   With the pack this was still arduous
although I made the two-mile hike in under
an hour   The hut seemed deserted As I walked
down the hill towards the sheep pen the owner
   came out with Rex who barked up a storm
I showed him my hands so he barked into them
at tremendous volume Nice rescue dog but
he did not like conscious strangers   The owner
     was hunting mushrooms
so he walked a way with me   When he saw
the horses on the abandoned ski slope
   he made a loud crying like
a mountain lion and the horses raced into
the woods   He picked mushrooms
and I continued on towards the ridge

After an hour on the middle ridge I stopped
and started my howl survey where
I pretended to be a wolf communicating
with young wolves—it worked in Alaska but here
it did not seem to fool them or inspire them
to answer even if they knew it was not a real
wolf   After three sets and no answers
   since July I walked on
The walk was very nice   The beech trees were
dropping their leaves and last nuts as I walked under
the canopy   Then after fording three streams
I came out into the fields   I could see the hut
from two ridges away so I slowed down
as the sun still had an hour on its metered
descent   I walked by a herd of horses grazing
near the cheese factory   Then I arrived
at the new night blind

I left my pack inside and went to an old
    roof of a cow shelter and took
a long piece of rubber—the roof was rubber
nailed like sheets of asphalt   This I put
on the wooden floor in the blind
    I put the sleeping bag over that
I went for a walk to the spring and counted
footprints then walked up the hill to watch
the setting sun   It had been a while
since I had done that   I lay down
on the grass and watched   It was sudden
since it went behind a mountain   The light
lasted for another hour   The fog and clouds
were rolling up from the north and covering
    everything   A large hawk swooped
down for a mouse and glided off into the fog

I walked back to the blind
and napped until dark   No moon
    tonight   I had the binoculars
scope flashlight camera and penknife
laid out on the edge of the window   The night
was uneventful The night scope did not
    work well beyond thirty meters in
the moonless night   I saw movements
and heard sounds but was not able to make
positive identifications   The owl was back
The stars were very bright   unusually so

Naturally I was up early despite alternating
hours dozing and observing   I observed
for another hour then wolfed down
an oat bar   I met the trail back up the hill
    After an hour of walking
through fields as I was about to enter
the beech forest I heard moans perhaps
from an elk   Not having heard
    an elk in weeks I wondered
if it could be a bear   So I walked directly
towards it   In the woods it was quiet

he has heard me whoever   Then after
a ridge I hear a light barking like a fox but
it became quiet also as I approached   The rest
of the walk was quiet   except
for some weasel scat nicely placed on rocks
for me to see and a little horse manure
          Not many signs today
The trip down was tiring but quick   I retrieved
the bike and coasted down the hill—my favorite
part   Soon I met Andrei with Bulchru
and Dimitar still cutting wood for winter.

Wild Cat Ghost

Measured movement
stillness under trees
          swift teeth
and a measured end for her

Connection between things
the pervading scent of life
present when spirits
     have moved on
and the shell remains

The corpse moved suddenly—
a buzzing horde
of yellowjackets
under her perfect fur—
     Can a ghost call a storm
or does the missing heart?

Snow Blind

Tsonyo was right on time at 6:30 in an extremely
old Lada   We drove to Vidima and met
Bulchru at the cafe where we all had tea
and croissants   Everyone complained
about the weather which was snowing lightly
and was expected to continue until Friday.
We left then for the base at the water plant
Then they parted saying 'good seeing' and headed
   up the ridge   I hiked directly to the hut
The trail was covered with snow and leaves
so footing was precarious   I took an hour
   and I was sweating
despite the snow   I was getting very weary
of carrying full backpacks everywhere.

No one was at the hizha so I had tea then checked
into a room for three days   It was the same
room Seven that I always
had   I turned off the small electric heater
before it burned down the building   I left
   for the mountain but it was so cold
with a northerly wind that I turned back
and put on long underwear and an extra wool cap
As I went into the woods I read many stories
in the snow   A wild swine had crossed the trail
   about a mile up and a fox had followed it for
a while before veering back on the trail.

A hundred meters further a roe deer had crossed
and the fox had followed her also for a while
then keeping to the trail otherwise.

Suddenly I was out of the forest but in a cloud
    of blowing snow   The path went through
many rock crags then it was in a long field
and wandered horizontally along the slope west
for several kilometers   I had to pass four frozen
streams and waterfalls which were difficult
to cross since the ice was covered with snow
Then the trail turned south and straight up
    the mountain   The wind was at my back
which helped going uphill   My lungs were starting
to freeze   Visibility worsened
Then I was on the level and going gently downhill
then uphill again   I could not see the mountain
    I knew it was to my left from seeing
it on a clear day   Some trail poles
but they were leading down again and I knew
that had to be wrong so I turned west and started
up what I thought was the base but now the wind
    was cutting through my two caps
one with a face mask which was solid ice
from my breath slobber and mucus   I huddled
        behind a post and repositioned
the caps   My watch pointed to almost One
If I got to the top then I would need shelter
for the night   If none then I was screwed
    so after a rest huddled in a ball
I turned back and followed my disappearing
footprints   I ran down the slope slipping and sliding
to get out of the wind   After an hour
or so I was below the hard winds
and the snow fell off   I was below
the clouds and could see Aprilci and the ridges.
I tried to take a few pictures
but the camera seemed to be frozen.

Chess Pieces

On the horizontal trail again I stopped
behind a rock and had a few peanuts   My lungs
and throat hurt I lay back and looked
   at the curtains of clouds blowing
over   I saw wolf prints that were now covering
my tracks—I had been followed   But I did
     not see how I could have passed
the wolf   The prints seemed small
a female I guessed   I looked up and saw
the spectacular landscape   I walked
out to a huge outcropping and lay down
on the snowy grasses and watched clouds
   Two sun beams focused on Aprilci   then
two chess pieces resolved themselves
in the rocks before me the king with his sunlit crown
tilted down facing the queen her blocky jaw
open in conversation or lecture below a pinhead
   I watched as the sun changed their aspects
enough to bring them alive then
   they were gone

I walked back on the real trail noticing
that I had been two meters above it on the way
out Then in the outcroppings I rested again
It was almost Four and I had to be careful
to return in the light although I did remember
the flashlight this time   In the woods
I rested one more time on a large fallen

beech tree   Looking back with the binoculars
I thought I saw movement in the trees wondering
if it was the wolf—perhaps she thought
        I was wounded
and about to be carrion   Good odds I felt
but not today as it was all downhill from here
I reached the hut before dark and immediately
had water tea and coke   No one was there
only the three employees painting the kitchen
The hot water machine was broken so
they put a pot on the wood stove which heated
the large dining room   From the room
I could see part of my trail under the clouds
before darkness erased the view   The mountain
was still hidden   I crawled into the sleeping
bag with long underwear and slept.

Sun on Snow
Despite my good intention to leave early
I was still asleep at Seven   But I went downstairs
for tea and croissant and was out the door
by Eight   The sky was clear and the sun
was peaking over the ridge   As I repeated
the first leg of the trip through the woods
I noticed that the wolf
        had followed me back
towards the hut yesterday   It was sunny
but with a cold breeze   Through the crags
and into the field   I decided to change
my direction to go west first   I saw
faint signs of a trail going straight up
the closest mountain so I decided to take it
and then cross over to the ridge trail
to Mount Botev and avoid
the boulder-strewn ravines

After an hour of going straight up through
rock slides and in snow I realized
it was a bad decision   Unfortunately
going down looked more dangerous

than continuing up   so I continued
up   At the first sub-peak was a cable
   stretching all the way up   fastened
every three meters with iron posts   This made
it easier to climb but my hands started freezing
to the posts   As I got higher the wind increased
and the snow started blowing   I could never
see the peak   only the nearest sub-peak—
   I accidentally surprised a mouse into a hole
Then I noticed a lot of mouse tracks leading
into holes   No wolf or fox prints so only hawks
and eagles would be threats   It was hard to breathe
my heart was racing so I slowed down
to a crawl   Sometimes the rocks
were so steep I had to leave the cable
and crawl around   other times I could pull
myself up with the cable.

Looking towards Mt. Botev

Fox Peak

Finally I was at the local crest   To the west
     was another peak, Ambaritsa, so
I walked in that direction for a while scanning
the area with binoculars   Then I turned back
and looked at Botev which was slightly higher
The walking was easy now   The wind gusted
When it stopped I lay down and had a few
peanuts   I could see the Sredna Gora mountain
range which paralleled the Stara Planina
     (Old Mountains)   They were dark
while these were coated with snow   At the top
was nine centimeters of snow   The trail
was well-marked   Soon I came upon prints
     of a hare and shortly afterwards
the prints of two foxes following   The foxes
veered off after the hare but returned and seemed
     to head for Botev   I stopped and took
photographs in all directions   Before I got to
Botev the trail dipped a few hundred meters
into a pass   I could see the trail posts leading
to the south   then I found some footprints
from yesterday   my own from the boot
pattern   Botev had been in clouds but these blew
off as I watched   The wind had picked up
I saw chamois prints in the pass.

Watching Chamois

I decided to climb Botev again   Again
the wind was at my back but it was cold
and I was getting tired It was maybe
    one o'clock—my watch seemed
to have frozen   I started the ascent
What I thought was an easy trail
from a distance was an eroded gully
treacherous with boulders and rock slides
Since it had less snow I climbed in the gully
stopping four times to curl up and rest
partially out of the wind   Finally
    I was on the peak
I thought I saw a tan chamois on the next
ridge over but too much blowing
snow and I could not locate it with binoculars
I looked around the peak   There were two
radio towers which looked like missiles
doubtless on purpose since it was a military
installation for forty years   I saw no
signs of activity   The buildings were closed
and locked even the one that looked like
a hizha   I walked around but the wind
and blowing snow were bitter
      It was difficult
to see and my tracks were already obliterated
    I stumbled into the wind   Suddenly
I realized that my right hand was
    frozen to my cap
and the fingers could not be moved
I tore it off from the cap and rammed
it in my pocket   Gradually as I tried to dive
    down the slope the fingers thawed
little one first   Again I was racing
to get out of the blowing snow.

Tracking the Tracker
Back in the pass I took the route
from yesterday   No wind made it into the pass
so I walked slowly   I saw movement
on the slope under the peak   Through
the binoculars I saw a female chamois black
instead of tan   She saw me and started to run
up the slope   I watched for a while then walked
     briskly down slope When I was lower
she stopped doubtless calculating
that I could never catch her from below
          Shortly I came upon a table rock
in the sun and stretched out
     I watched her through
the glasses   She grazed for a while then I lost
her   She had been rolling in the snow
and got up   Then grazed some more
     on the grasses   I had a few peanuts
then took some snow off the grasses
beside me and swallowed it
for moisture   I made whistling noises
but possibly she could not see me
on the rock or hear the noises
          on the north wind

After a good rest I walked down the trail
and through the cuts through the ridges
On the horizontal trail I could see that
     the wolf had followed
my trip back yesterday
afternoon also   Every so often wherever
another trail crossed was fresh scat   I found
one more set of chamois prints that led
directly up the slope
     but could not identify sex
          Mouse prints on the trail
fresh   one continued for almost two hundred
meters quite a long way for a mouse   At one
of the waterfalls I lost
my balance on the ice   fell
and started to slide

down the steep frozen stream   I stopped by
grabbing a rough patch   but pulled
a tendon   I crawled to the side
where it was just rock   Uncomfortable
to walk or climb   Back through
the crags and into the forest
the trees were rimed
with snow and ice and all were white
    In the forest it was calmer   I rested
one last time on a downed beech
cleaning snow off my jeans and boots

The sun was setting behind the range

I limped the last slope down
to the hut   It was almost dark
I hauled myself to the bar
and had cold water and a coke
I hung my coat and sweater in front
    of the stove   Then to bed and the sleep
of the dead   or innocent

Imaginary Wolves

Waiting for Wolves

Prints like black words
　　　　　　　on a page
　　　divide the mud
　　　　　　　what kind of history
is written in prints
　　　in mud, hair stuck in sap
on a pine?

What if I discover
　　　　　　　that judgment depends
on a home lair
　　　　　that can be reclaimed
and not by knowledge
　　　　　　　　of the evolution of stars
or words with political
　　　　　savvy?

Lead to the conclusion—a foot
and spine of the boar
white beyond the snow
　　　black hairs
　　like seeds of
spontaneous regeneration

The Passion of Wolves

Veils of fog　veils for
　　the bride whose
trail of hot-blooded prints goes around
in circles while the male makes
　　larger circles around
until the circles overlap in place.

Who's world is this?　Not mine
　　Hers a deeper world
whose dimensions and depth
　　　leave me flat
　　I've seen no wolves

but feel the spirit infused
on every blade or crumb of dirt.
Now I am just an extra image
another threat to be avoided.
The uncertain ice the dangerous weather
    the uncertain prey

      A voice rises
it is pure singing made more pure
by distance and untouchableness
My mouth opens in response
but I cannot participate
it would have no meaning
    to them   so I listen

Closer to the lair is more silence
I finally find that I cannot go
there   it is not my place
I need not know
    immediately
I can wait and watch   and listen
       and learn
From my rough shelter
I thought of their shelter
lined and warmer

Paths appear paths open

I understand the levels that combine
to bring my hearing a small 'swuff'
from the oxidation to the mitochondria
    viruses   cells

only I am foolish enough
to wrestle with thunder and conscience
    others are home asleep
Without distractions I am more alive
uncomfortable   cold   hungry
but I have bread and water
      chocolate in my pockets

Old Wolf Song

I am wolf.
I chase deer who chase
grass who chase the sun—grass
is light deer are light wolf is light

Across asia siberia america europe
I chase deer and mice and light.
Not alone no always in a family
always at home. I was raised by my parents
my aunts uncles brothers sisters. I learned
the cycle of heat the meaning of clouds
the feel of grass the scent of prey
the culture of our ways how to play
and rest and play.

I learned to hunt with my brothers and sisters
and with ravens and men for we all had
different needs and could share a game.

I found a mate. We played shared mice
and moons and fluids. Our way of mating
is beyond you—we hold and hold until
we are dry and fall apart. We made
a den then cubs came from us
and we joyed in their presence
and the presence of friends who helped
us raise them teaching them how to play
how to find and eat rest and play.
And sleep and play and play.

We were many a populous people
until you came other men in greater numbers
with sharper teeth and faster claws
to take our food take out homes.
You pushed us from the day light.
There were fewer places fewer pups
fewer of us. Then none. Deer and elk
have no one to keep them healthy.
And light has one less facet.

I am wolf. I am old and stiff
I need to piss—ah, howl
with me one more time for the missing
now.

Wolf News

This is what I see: tracks,
lines, bent stalks, small prints
in dirt—but there are primary trails:
The standing scents of trees   rocks   streams
slight vapors   and the clouds of smell   the history
of all who passed before me   their mood
and direction   health and intent   messages
that cannot go unread   only evaporate
and be replaced by newer ones   layer
upon layer of deep rich sediment   exhalations
urinations   oils   saliva   hairs   excretions
the signs that let me taste who ranks   who rejects
who mates   or not   who travels
who kills   who sickens
who is at home   who is not
whatever is dropped
brushed   torn   left behind
whatever can be carried by wind and air
and can tell me the story
of the hour   whatever I can use
to complete my own needs
and understanding   though there
are things I do not know—how do butterflies die?
do they just land   fold their wings
and wait   not to fly
again?   does time slow   or being extend?
My own death may not be as easy
but you can taste that story later.

The Shepherd's Song to the She-wolf
I have brought you this lard
for your health so you will not eat
my sheep but I have added a special elixir
that will make your belly hard
and tight as when you know the love
of a male but not love nor water nor food
will cure this poison You will fall
and lay and gasp and twitch at the art
I have employed to stop your heart
to stop you preying on my flock
and when you are dead and stiff
I shall parade around you cut your fur
and take it and wrap it around me—all
because of one sheep I could not find.

The She-wolf's Reply to the Shepherd
I do not take gifts even for the health
of my pups   The gifts are deadly
as gifts from your kind have ever been.
    I am skilled at finding the weakest
prey or the slowest youngest oldest.
I prefer the taste of deer but I will eat
mice cheflik beetles and if they die
nearby parts of dogs cows or sheep.
Your flesh is not to my liking so
    I do not kill or eat you humans.
Ignore me and I keep to our tradition.
I do not deserve your deadly attention
which needs to be on your flock
    so it does not wander or sicken
in the heat. I only take what is offered
and do not ask for more. If you leave
    us alone the health of your flock
and my pack should both increase.

Biologist's Plan

I had to invade your place
and analyze it. I had to kill
    you to see what things you ate.
I had to measure your timing
to understand—perhaps
I could have waited and watched
but there were time limits
    for my grant.

And I wanted to save you
by proving you increased the health
    of your prey
and now that I have made models
from all I've captured and weighed
I can prove your species
      is critical to the whole
and I can rest superior
    in my myths.

Looking towards the Stara Planina

Still Snake
The snake does not
    move—it cannot. I see
the wound   human

Animals know
       and refuse to live
vultures wait alone
   and frogs die in ponds
rivers of life run dry

Feelings frozen in masks
      the lines slip
out of focus—exhaustion
      transformed to vision
a last perfect order
  on a deepening red horizon

The mind craves harmony
    the heart only quiet.

Alpha Reasoning
Wolves are perfect size midway between
the cause of the sneeze and the elk
    who sneezes.
humans are too big much to
big to fit comfortably—
wolf is halfway between shrews
and whales
a perfect size—humans
are too big to be optimal.

To the question: what is the perfect size?
    Wolf is the answer.
Only we have time to howl
only we have time to sit or play
or lie still   only we let all things be
    except for the little we need.

Howling

I heard howling
again—some things were meant
   to be sung

Scat—it is not the discovery
of an ocean or people
   but it signifies

Nothing is white   not the snow
or clouds or air   but
     shades of blue   grey
with yellows   greens in the distance

   Now I am in time
and my soul expands to examine
the trees and grasses   the roots
and dead branches   leaves
and the further it goes
from me the greater
     the joy

The corridors of sounds   like the roads
of dreams   lead to expanded
horizons.

Claw Marks

I saw the claw marks
on my arms   knew the teeth
of the bear were waiting in the shadow
   on the hill
I paced the tracks   hair
standing on end

This evening   no one
   is sleeping
But how could death come from so many
beings who only avoid me as they go about eating?
Always the sense of the presence
   of death is here

The knife flashes in
candlelight   as I cut bread
then whittle to think
    about the day.
I keep this knife thinking
it is my claw for defense

Walking back to the village
through the olive trees
I play with the knife
    slave to an idea
that I can save wolves
    protect myself
learn how they live
live simply myself
it is all I have left of technical hybrids

At first I saw all nature as what
    I had learned
the proof of theories or guesses
then it was a mirror
that showed me the whole
with my self
    embedded.

So much space not filled with me
    or human design
anger released into those spaces
so the mountains become
more important than the image
    the social mask
(the human city is the barren
archetype   not the mountain)

I have not seen the wolf
with certainty   met his face
or weighed him
but we have had
    a conversation
filled with exchanges and absences
information traded from our

scents and tracks

Wolf was never mine   nor was the mountain
    even the memories.
Here is one thing I learned
that his world has little connection with mine
and the human world is just a restraint
   on his free motion

We circulated on the same
paths that had their direct logic

When I am here all the feelings
   find release
the irony—that more words
might save wolves
   if people hear them.

Passions of Wolf

The blood is not any hotter than mine is
    mammal blood after all
the lust for life is no stronger
than what I feel.

But then I am not a wolf
not even in my imagination
then I shiver and my mind
   seizes on a smell drifting
up the valley   It is a human smell
burning   a camp fire perhaps.

I unconsciously turn away
I am thirsty   I want to run
no not run   chase
   something with blood
as hot as mine to have that blood
pass my lips and make
it mine. To taste
        that life.

Seeing Light

For years I have tracked and chased
through mud and snow   in rain and sun
        I have waited and watched.

What have I seen? Every animal but
            one.
Crossed paths with bears   and wild pigs
    followed hares and mice.

Seen every facet of sunlight on leaves
every shade of blue on the mountains
Seen everything that a wolf has seen

So many words   so many hours waiting
        For the flash of recognition
For the moment of face-to-face
            and in all the years
Only a fleeting green shape at night
From a distance

So little to reflect   to reflect on
        and still the outpouring of words
surrounding the topic
    but not touching it
        not sharing the place
or perhaps sharing but not occupying
it at the same time.

Lightbearer

    I absorb light
from the sun during
the day or at least
        make it internal so
it can carry taste
and sound. At night
        release it so I can see
during the rare
    times I can shed

the verbal embrace
and not think or try to speak
I can still see. I am less
                and less human
        the pulse of blood
quiets and slows

then I am dark
    not as a shadow
or the absence of light
    but dark as the space where
light has never reached
    at the edge of being
        or in my empty heart.

Wolf Loves to Hide
Nature loves to hide
    and nature loves to play
play at hiding
        hide while playing
        display
    show and turn
and expect you to remember

        We remember
even as we see
again and the present
    expands

Nature loves to hide and tease
but wolves love to seek
and humans love to seek and please

And so we seek each other and play
    And hide within nature
our nature   her nature   his nature
all the natures that exist—

About the author

Yulalona Leelannee Lopez was educated in astrophysics at Harvard University and is associated with the Tohono O'odham. To earn a living for the past ten years, her vocation has been investing in commodities; she lives in Grants Pass, Oregon. Her avocation is saving places and cultures, working through The Nature Conservancy, Cultural Survival, and other groups. She is a founding member of the Palouse Poets Collective and a contributor to Nieman Ryan Community Designs.

She writes as a passion, to persuade others to her views. Although she has published individual poems in journals, this is her second book. She explains: "Mostly, when I read other poets, I think that they didn't study enough astronomy, didn't get their knees scratched trying to follow earthworms, haven't caught cold watching it snow on their hands, haven't shaped their body to the bole of a tree or crawled along a deer path through thickets—bend or become still or small. I want to speak to these nonhuman experiences." Her name 'Yulalona' is from the Modoc meaning 'water blown backwards by the wind against the river current.'

Colophon

This book is set in Palatino using Indesign on a Macintosh Ibook in the mountain village of Vidima near the Severen Djendem region in the continental zone during a cool spring between wolf surveys.

Photographs of Bulgarian and Serbian sites
by Y. L. Lopez and Angel Vulkov

Book and Cover design by Rian Ektropic Designs